RAINBOW magic ®

The Fun Day Fairies

For Evie Newberry,
with lots of love

Special thanks to
Narinder Dhami

ORCHARD BOOKS
338 Euston Road, London NW1 3BH
Orchard Books Australia
Hachette Children's Books
Level 17/207 Kent Street, Sydney, NSW 2000
A Paperback Original

First published in Great Britain in 2006
Rainbow Magic is a registered trademark of Working Partners Limited.
Series created by Working Partners Limited, London W6 OQT

Text © Working Partners Limited 2006
Illustrations © Georgie Ripper 2006
The right of Georgie Ripper to be identified as the illustrator
of this work has been asserted by her in accordance
with the Copyright, Designs and Patents Act, 1988.
A CIP catalogue record for this book is available
from the British Library.

ISBN 1 84616 190 8
1 3 5 7 9 10 8 6 4 2

Printed in Great Britain

Willow
the Wednesday Fairy

by Daisy Meadows

illustrated by Georgie Ripper

ORCHARD BOOKS

www.rainbowmagic.co.uk

Icy wind now fiercely blow!
To the Time Tower I must go.
Goblin servants follow me
And steal the Fun Day Flags I need.

I know there will be no fun,
For fairies or humans once the flags are gone.
So, storm winds, take me where I say.
My plan for chaos starts today!

Contents

Arts and Crafts   9

Bits and Pieces   21

Artistic Goblins   33

Butterfly Fun   47

A Lasting Impression   55

Fairy Painting   67

Arts and Crafts

"This is great, Kirsty!" Rachel Walker said, beaming at her best friend, Kirsty Tate, as they wandered around the Tippington Community Centre Arts and Crafts Fair. "I don't know what to try first!"

The fair was in full swing. Wooden tables covered with long white cloths had been placed in a huge square, and each table had been set up for different crafts. Rachel and Kirsty could see neat piles of velvet, satin and silk fabrics for patchwork on one table, and knitting needles and baskets of fluffy wool on another. At one corner of the square,

a man was demonstrating origami,
and Mrs Walker, Rachel's mum,
was running the scrapbooking stall.
Each table had space for people to
try the crafts themselves, and there
were already long queues at some
of them.

"It's fantastic, isn't it?" Kirsty agreed, looking around. "And I've just thought of something: with so much colourful fabric and paper about, this would be the perfect place to find one of the fairies' Fun Day Flags!"

"You're right!" Rachel agreed. "And it's Wednesday today, so we should look out for Willow's Wednesday flag."

Kirsty and Rachel shared a wonderful secret. They were friends with the fairies, and had often helped their tiny friends when icy Jack Frost and his mean goblin servants caused trouble. Now the fairies had asked the girls to help them find the seven magical flags which the Fun Day Fairies used to recharge their magic, so that every day of the week could be filled with fun.

Jack Frost and his goblins had stolen the flags, but the Fun Day Magic had made the goblins even more mischievous than usual! Furious at the goblins' antics, Jack Frost had cast a spell to banish the flags to the human world. But the goblins missed the flags' fun effects, so they sneaked away to try and get them back. Now the fairies were relying on Rachel and Kirsty to help them find the flags before the goblins did.

"I hope we can find all the Fun Day Flags before I have to go home at the end of half-term," Kirsty said. Then she noticed that Rachel was frowning.

"What's the matter?" she asked.

"Have you noticed that no one looks very excited?" Rachel whispered, pointing at the visitors filling the room.

Kirsty looked around. Rachel was right; although some people were smiling, nobody looked as if they were really having much fun. "That's because Willow's Wednesday Flag is missing," Kirsty sighed.

Rachel nodded. "And it's going to be hard to spot the flag with so many people around," she pointed out.

"Remember what the Fairy Queen always says," Kirsty reminded her. "We have to let the magic come to us."

Rachel smiled. "You're right," she said. "Which craft shall we try first?"

"Look, there's no queue at the jewellery-making stall," Kirsty pointed out. "Let's go there."

The girls hurried over to the stall. The table was covered in bracelets, necklaces and earrings, all made of sparkling beads in many different colours.

"Hello, girls," the stallholder said, smiling. "Would you like to make some bracelets?"

"Yes, please," Kirsty replied.

She and Rachel sat down and the man gave each of them scissors, string and a silver clasp.

"Cut the string to fit your wrist," he explained, as he pulled out a large plastic box with lots of little drawers from under the table. "And then thread these beads onto your string to make your bracelet. You're welcome to use any of the beads you like."

Rachel and Kirsty measured each other's wrists and cut their strings, as the man moved away to talk to another stallholder. Then, eagerly, they opened the tiny drawers.

"Ooh, these are lovely!" Rachel gasped, as they found different-sized beads in all the colours of the rainbow.

The girls began threading beads onto their bracelets. Rachel was using sparkly beads of all different sizes, while Kirsty had chosen tiny pink and purple ones.

Soon Kirsty realised that the drawer of small pink beads was emptying rapidly, and she still had the last bit of her bracelet to finish. She began checking the drawers she hadn't opened yet, hoping there might be more pink beads somewhere.

Suddenly, Kirsty's heart skipped
a beat. A faint glittery green sparkle
was swirling around one of the drawers.
Kirsty gently pulled the drawer open,
peeped inside and there sat a tiny fairy
smiling up at her!

"Rachel," Kirsty whispered happily.
"It's Willow the Wednesday Fairy!"

Bits and Pieces

Willow looked thrilled to see the
girls. She wore a floaty dress with
a handkerchief-point hem in different
shades of green, from light to dark,
and little green slippers on her feet.

"Hello, Willow," Rachel said.
"Have you come because the
Wednesday flag is here somewhere?"

Willow peeped cautiously out of the drawer. The stallholder was facing the other way as he chatted to the woman at the potter's wheel, so Willow leapt lightly out of the box and hovered in front of the girls.

"Yes, Rachel," she declared. "I think my flag is here. And the poem in the Book of Days will help us find it."

The Book of Days was looked
after by Fairyland's Royal Time
Guard, Francis the frog. Every
morning Francis checked which day
it was in the Book of Days, and
then ran the correct Fun Day Flag
up the flagpole at the top of the
Time Tower. When the sun hit the
Fun Day Flag, the magical rays
would shine down into the courtyard
where a fairy would be waiting to
charge her wand with Fun Day
Magic. Since the flags had been
stolen, poems had magically
appeared in the Book of Days,
giving clues as to where each flag
might be.

"Tell us the poem, Willow," Kirsty
said eagerly.

Willow began to recite:

"Yards of fabric, strings of beads
Follow the glitter, see where it leads.
It once was one but now it's three;
The Wednesday Flag means fun and glee!"

"'It once was one but now it's three',"
Rachel repeated. "What does that mean?"

"I don't know," Kirsty replied. "But I think perhaps the first bit means we have to follow a trail of glitter."

Willow nodded. "But first, let me finish your bracelets for you." She lifted her wand and a shower of emerald sparkles floated down onto the two bracelets. Immediately, more beads magically appeared to finish both bracelets, and the clasps jumped neatly into place.

The stallholder was coming back, so Willow quickly zoomed over to hide in Rachel's pocket. Meanwhile, the girls put their bracelets on.

"Look," Willow whispered, leaning
out of Rachel's pocket and pointing at
the floor with her wand. "Glitter!"

Rachel and Kirsty looked down and
saw a small pile of gold glitter on the
floor near the jewellery stall.

"It's not really a trail of glitter,
though, is it?" Kirsty said doubtfully.
"Just a heap."

"There's a button and some ribbon next to it," Willow pointed out.

"And another pile of glitter a bit further on," Rachel added.

The girls thanked the stallholder for their bracelets and then hurried over to the second heap of glitter. Now they could see that there was a higgledy-piggledy trail of glitter, buttons, ribbons, fabric and beads.

"Where does it lead?" Willow whispered eagerly.

Rachel and Kirsty carefully followed the glitter trail. It led them right up to the quilting stall, where several people were sewing different pieces of brightly coloured fabric onto a beautiful patchwork quilt.

At that moment a woman put down her needle and reached for a new piece of fabric. Rachel and Kirsty noticed that the fabric squares were stacked neatly in piles at one side of the table. And on top of one pile was a piece of beautiful golden cloth with glittery patches.

Rachel nudged Kirsty. "The pattern on that gold material looks just like the pattern on the Fun Day Flags," she murmured. "But it can't be Willow's flag, can it?"

"I don't think so," Kirsty agreed, frowning. "It looks much smaller than the other flags we've found."

Willow peeped out to look at the gold material. As soon as she saw it a big smile lit up her face. "It is my flag!" she whispered. "Well, part of it, anyway. Remember that the poem said 'It once was one but now it's three'?

It must have meant that my flag is now in three pieces."

"Oh, no!" Kirsty exclaimed in horror. "You mean the flag has been ruined? Whatever can we do?"

Artistic Goblins

"Don't worry," Willow replied quickly. "As long as we can find all three pieces, I can make the flag as good as new with my fairy magic."

The three friends stared longingly at the piece of the flag lying on the table. The woman running the stall saw them looking and smiled.

"That's a lovely fabric, isn't it?" she remarked.

Rachel nodded as an idea popped into her head. "Do you think I could have it for a project I'm doing?" she asked. "I'll pay for it."

"Oh, you're welcome to it, my dear," the woman replied. "And I think we have some more pieces of that cloth somewhere." She turned away and began hunting around the table.

Kirsty and Rachel glanced at each other in delight. Were they going to get all three pieces of Willow's flag back at once? But to the girls' disappointment, the woman came back empty-handed.

"I'm sorry," she said, frowning, "I can't find anymore. I remember I had a large piece originally and I cut it up earlier today." She picked up the one piece of the flag and handed it to Rachel. "We haven't used any in the quilt yet, so I don't know where the other bits have got to."

"Thank you," Rachel said gratefully, tucking the material safely into her pocket. Then she turned back to Kirsty, looking anxious. "Where are we going to look for the other pieces?" she asked.

But Kirsty was staring at the floor. "It's OK," she told Rachel. "The glitter trail keeps going. Look!"

"Brilliant," Rachel said with relief.

"Let's go!" Willow added happily.

Eagerly the friends began following
the sparkly glitter trail again. Along
with the glitter, they saw broken
crayons, pompoms and embroidery silks.
This time the trail led them to the
origami table, where people were
learning how to fold paper into
colourful fish, flowers and birds.

"Kirsty, the glitter trail goes under the tablecloth!" Rachel whispered.

"Do you think the trail carries on under there?" Kirsty asked.

Rachel lifted a corner of the tablecloth to check. To her surprise, she saw four big green feet hurrying past. Goblins! Cautiously, she lifted the tablecloth a little further and peered at the two goblins. They were carrying huge piles of cloth, paper and glue in their arms, and they were far too busy muttering gleefully to each other to notice Rachel. The

goblins hurried along under the row
of stalls, completely hidden by the
long tablecloths.

"There are goblins under the
tables!" Rachel whispered. Kirsty's
eyes opened wide, and Willow, who
was peeping out of Rachel's pocket,
gasped in surprise.

"I bet they're up to mischief!" Kirsty said.

"And looking for the Wednesday flag!" Willow added. "Maybe they have some of the missing pieces."

"We'd better follow them," suggested Kirsty. "But we'll have to be fairy-sized to do that."

Rachel glanced around. "There are too many people about," she said.

"Look," Willow whispered, pointing her wand at a dressmaking stall. "There's a screen there for trying on clothes."

"Perfect!" Kirsty exclaimed. She and Rachel hurried over and slipped behind the screen while no one was looking.

Willow immediately flew out of Rachel's pocket and showered the girls with sparkling fairy dust. In the twinkling of an eye, Rachel and Kirsty were tiny fairies with shining wings.

"Now we must fly low," Willow warned, "and get underneath the nearest table as fast as we can!"

The girls followed Willow as she
fluttered out from behind the screen,
and dodged the legs of people clustered
at the sewing table. Finally they darted
safely under the tablecloth out of sight.

"This way," Rachel said, pointing in
the direction the goblins had taken.

They flew along slowly along
underneath the square of tables, careful
to avoid the boxes and bags which
were stored there.

"I can hear giggling," Kirsty whispered.

Willow nodded. "That's a goblin giggle," she said confidently. She beckoned to the girls and they flew behind a large plastic storage box. Then they all peeped carefully out from behind it.

The goblins were sitting underneath the next table. They had collected all sorts of art materials and were sticking them onto a big piece of cardboard. Willow and the girls could see buttons, beads, wool, bits of material and patterned papers scattered around them.

"The goblins are making a collage!" Willow murmured.

The goblins were clearly having great fun as they rummaged through their craft supplies. They chattered happily to each other as they threw things aside that they didn't want to use. Buttons, beads, pompoms and coloured papers went flying. One of the goblins tossed away a piece of pink and silver paper, which landed on the floor at Kirsty's feet. She could see that it was a beautiful butterfly from the origami table.

"Look!" Rachel gasped, her voice full of excitement. She was pointing at the goblin's heap of supplies. "I can see another section of Willow's Wednesday flag!"

Butterfly Fun

Kirsty and Willow looked too, and saw the piece of sparkly gold material among the goblins' things.

"That's why the goblins are having so much fun!" Willow said.

Rachel frowned. "If they knew they had part of the flag, surely they'd be taking better care of it?"

she said thoughtfully.

"You're right!" Willow agreed.
"Which can only mean that the goblins
are so silly, they don't know what
they've got! Maybe we can get it back
before they notice."

"We need to lure the goblins away so
we can grab it," Kirsty said. She
glanced down at the origami butterfly
at her feet. "I've got an idea!"

Quickly Kirsty whispered her plan to
Willow. The fairy smiled and raised her
wand, sending a few sparkles of fairy
magic drifting down
onto the delicate
paper butterfly.

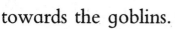

Kirsty and
Rachel
watched as
the butterfly
began to beat
its pink and
silver wings.
Then it
fluttered up
into the air
and danced
gracefully
towards the goblins.

The first goblin glanced up as the butterfly came closer. His eyes opened wide in fascination, and he nudged the other goblin in the ribs. "Look, a beautiful flutterby!" he said. The second goblin looked up and noticed the butterfly too. "Ooh, yes," he agreed. "Look at its shiny wings!"

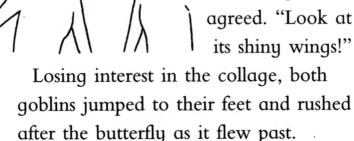

Losing interest in the collage, both goblins jumped to their feet and rushed after the butterfly as it flew past.

"Come on!" Willow whispered.

The friends hurried over to the pile of beads, buttons and bric-a-brac. Willow waved her wand above the piece of flag, and it immediately shrank so that Rachel could tuck it into her pocket.

"Now we've got two pieces!" Rachel said happily.

The goblins hadn't noticed because they were trying to catch the butterfly.

"Where have you come from, flutterby?" the first goblin asked, reaching out for it. This time he caught it, but as soon as he touched it, Willow's magic disappeared and the butterfly became a piece of paper again.

Willow and the girls couldn't help laughing at the look of amazement on both goblins' faces.

"You broke it!" the second goblin wailed, while the first goblin unfolded the paper, scratching his head as he tried to figure out what had made it fly.

"What now?" asked Kirsty.

"Look," Willow said, pointing at the floor. "There's more of the glitter trail!"

The girls and Willow flew on,

following the trail. It led them round a corner of the square of tables, and suddenly, there in front of them were two more goblins! They were marching along happily together, chatting and chuckling, and one of them was holding the last piece of the Wednesday flag in his hand!

A Lasting Impression

Quick as a flash, the friends dived
behind a large carrier bag, and peeped
out to see what the goblins were up to.

"Well, we've got one piece of the
flag, but what about the rest of it?"
the first goblin was saying.

"The others are too busy having
fun to look for the missing pieces,"

the second goblin giggled.

"We'd better go and remind them then," the first goblin said. Then he grinned. "We'll sneak up on them and shout BOO! That will frighten them out of their skins!"

"Ooh, good idea," the second goblin agreed, roaring with laughter.

"That piece of my flag means they're full of fun!" Willow whispered, as she and the girls watched the goblins heading off to find their friends. "We have to get that last piece back!"

Rachel and Kirsty thought hard.

Suddenly Rachel's face lit up.
"Maybe we can distract those two
goblins by helping them have some
more fun," she said. "I saw a big
tub of clay underneath the sculpture
table when we flew past. If we could
get the goblins to try making hand
impressions, they'd have to put the
flag down."

"That's a brilliant idea!"
Willow exclaimed in delight.

"We'll have to get back to the
sculpture table fast, though," Kirsty
pointed out. "The goblins are
already ahead of us!"

"How are we going to overtake
them without being seen?" asked
Rachel.

"We could slip out from underneath

the tables," Willow suggested, "fly
really fast along the outside, and then,
once we've overtaken the goblins, dive
under the tables again. We'll just have
to be careful that nobody spots us."

Rachel and Kirsty nodded
and followed Willow
out from under the
tablecloth. The little
fairy shot off so
fast, she was
almost a blur.
Rachel and Kirsty
zoomed after her,
dodging legs as
they wove their
way in and out of
the people around
the stalls.

Finally, Willow swooped underneath
the sculpture table, closely followed
by the girls. The big tub of clay
Rachel had noticed earlier was still
there and Kirsty could hear the
goblins approaching.

"We made it,"
Kirsty gasped.
"Here come the
goblins!"

"Argue with
me, Kirsty,"
Rachel said in
a low voice.
"I want to go first!"
she added loudly.

"No, me first! Me first!" Kirsty
protested, pretending to
glare at Rachel.

The goblins heard them and looked over at the girls curiously.

"It's very important to be first," Willow put in. "Maybe it should be me."

"It was my idea. I'll go first," Rachel argued.

"No! Me first!" one of the goblins snapped, marching over and elbowing Rachel aside.

"No, me!" the one with the flag yelled rudely, following his friend. Then he stared at the clay, looking puzzled. "What are you doing?"

"Putting our hands in the clay to make impressions of them," Kirsty explained.

"Let's have a go!" the first goblin said to his friend.

But the second goblin shook his head firmly. "I can't," he muttered, clutching the piece of flag tightly, "I have to hold this."

Kirsty and Rachel were dismayed, but Willow jumped in.

"Then why don't you do your
feet?" she suggested. "That
way, you won't have to
let go of anything."

The goblin's face
brightened. "Ooh,
yes!" he agreed.

Both goblins
climbed eagerly
onto the edge
of the tub.

"After three,"
Kirsty called.
"One – two
– THREE!"

The goblins jumped into
the clay and landed with
a splash, sinking down into it
a little way. Immediately, Willow

waved her wand and fairy dust
swirled around the tub.
"Hey!" the first goblin
shouted, trying to pull
one of his feet out
of the clay.
"I can't move!"
"The clay's set
hard!" roared
the second
goblin furiously,
swaying from
side to side as he
tried to escape.
"You tricked us!"
Laughing, Rachel
and Kirsty flew
over and pulled the
piece of flag easily from his hands.

Both goblins yelled and grumbled, but they couldn't do anything to stop the girls. Willow used her magic to shrink the flag fabric and Rachel put it in her pocket with the other bits.

"We've got all three pieces of
my Wednesday flag back at last!"
Willow declared, her eyes shining
with happiness.

Fairy Painting

"Let us go!" the goblins shrieked crossly as Willow and the girls flew away.

"My spell will wear off in a few minutes," Willow told Rachel and Kirsty. "But that will give me just enough time to put my flag back together and take it home to Fairyland."

Once they were safely out of sight of
the goblins, they stopped. Rachel took all
the pieces of the flag out of her pocket,
and she and Kirsty laid
them carefully out on the
floor. Then Willow
waved her wand,
and with a flash of
magic sparkles in
all the colours of the
rainbow, the flag was whole again.

"You can't tell it was ever cut up!"
Rachel said admiringly, staring at the
beautiful flag.

Willow nodded happily. Then she
grinned. "I'll have to make you human
again while we're out of sight under
here, girls," she said. "Mind you don't
hit your heads."

With another wave of her wand, Willow turned Rachel and Kirsty back to normal. The girls crouched on their knees, trying not to knock against the tabletop.

"Thank you, girls," Willow said. "I must go to Fairyland now and recharge my wand, but I'll be back very soon!" And, with that, she vanished in a mist of fairy dust.

Cautiously, Rachel and Kirsty crawled out from under the table, hoping no one would notice them.

"Girls!" Mrs Walker exclaimed.

Rachel and Kirsty looked up to see her standing staring down at them in amazement.

"What are you doing under my table?"

Rachel and Kirsty grinned at each other. They hadn't realised they were underneath Rachel's mum's stall!

"We were just helping to tidy up," Rachel said quickly, picking up some scissors she'd just noticed lying on the floor.

"We've been making bracelets," added Kirsty, standing up and showing hers to Rachel's mum.

"Oh, they're lovely!" Mrs Walker exclaimed, examining it. Then she glanced at her watch. "You know, there's still an hour to go before the fair closes. Why don't you have a go at something else?"

"OK," said Rachel. "Come on, Kirsty!"

"What shall we try next?" Kirsty asked as they wandered round the room.

"I've always wanted to have a go on a potter's wheel," Rachel said. "Or what about the embroidery table?"

"I don't mind," Kirsty replied. "I just hope Willow's managed to recharge her wand by now!"

"Psst!" came an urgent hiss.

Rachel and Kirsty stopped and looked around. Then, seeing a faint gleam of fairy magic round one of the tablecloths, they bent down and lifted the corner. There was Willow, hovering under the embroidery table.

"Hello, girls!" she beamed. "Look!" She waved her wand a couple

of times and Kirsty and Rachel saw
a stream of magical sparkles
flow underneath the tables,
swirling and zooming
from one to the other.
"I've recharged my wand
with Fun Day Magic.
Wednesday will be a lot more
fun from now on!" Willow promised.

Kirsty and Rachel glanced at each
other in delight.

"Everyone in Fairyland was thrilled,"
Willow went on, "and the King and
Queen and Francis told me to say well
done! Now I must be going, but," she
winked at the girls, "you might like to
try model-painting before you go home.
Goodbye!" And with another swirl of
fairy dust, Willow was gone.

"Model-painting?" Rachel said, glancing round the hall. "Where's that?"

"Over by the origami," said Kirsty, pointing.

The girls hurried to the table where people were sitting painting models of birds and animals.

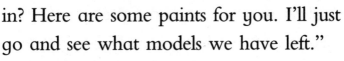

"Hello, girls," the woman running the stall said, smiling. "Would you like to join in? Here are some paints for you. I'll just go and see what models we have left."

Rachel and Kirsty found two empty seats. But the woman came back a few moments later, looking puzzled.

"I don't even remember packing these," she said. "But I seem to have lots, and I thought you might like them."

And she put two beautiful fairy models down on the table. Rachel and Kirsty could hardly believe their eyes.

"It must have been Willow's magic!" Rachel whispered, and Kirsty nodded.

"Here's some wire to make wings," the woman went on.

People standing around the stall were also starting to notice the pretty models.

"Mum, can I have a go?" asked one little girl.

"Me too!" said another eagerly.

Soon the table was full of people painting the delicate fairy models and fixing wire wings to their backs.

Everyone chattered
happily as more and
more people crowded
round to join in.

"We're not the only
people at the fair who
are having fun," Rachel
said to Kirsty, as they finished off their
models which they'd painted in different
shades of green to look like Willow.
"Look at all these smiling faces!"

Kirsty grinned. "Yes, Willow's Fun
Day Magic is working perfectly again,"
she agreed. "Let's hope we can make
tomorrow just as fun by finding
another flag!"

The Fun Day Fairies

Megan, Tallulah and Willow have
got their flags back. Now Rachel
and Kirsty must help

Thea the Thursday Fairy

Win Rainbow Magic goodies!

In every book in the Rainbow Magic Fun Day Fairies series (books 36-42) there is a hidden picture of a flag with a secret letter in it. Find all seven letters and re-arrange them to make a special Fairyland word, then send it to us. Each month we will put the entries into a draw and select one winner to receive a Rainbow Magic Sparkly T-shirt and Goody Bag!

Send your entry on a postcard to Rainbow Magic Fun Day Competition, Orchard Books, 338 Euston Road, London NW1 3BH. Australian readers should write to Hachette Children's Books, Level 17/207 Kent Street, Sydney, NSW 2000. Don't forget to include your name and address. Only one entry per child. Final draw: 30th September 2007.

Have you checked out the

website at:
www.rainbowmagic.co.uk

by Daisy Meadows

The Rainbow Fairies

Ruby the Red Fairy	ISBN	1 84362 016 2
Amber the Orange Fairy	ISBN	1 84362 017 0
Saffron the Yellow Fairy	ISBN	1 84362 018 9
Fern the Green Fairy	ISBN	1 84362 019 7
Sky the Blue Fairy	ISBN	1 84362 020 0
Izzy the Indigo Fairy	ISBN	1 84362 021 9
Heather the Violet Fairy	ISBN	1 84362 022 7

The Weather Fairies

Crystal the Snow Fairy	ISBN	1 84362 633 0
Abigail the Breeze Fairy	ISBN	1 84362 634 9
Pearl the Cloud Fairy	ISBN	1 84362 635 7
Goldie the Sunshine Fairy	ISBN	1 84362 641 1
Evie the Mist Fairy	ISBN	1 84362 636 5
Storm the Lightning Fairy	ISBN	1 84362 637 3
Hayley the Rain Fairy	ISBN	1 84362 638 1

The Party Fairies

Cherry the Cake Fairy	ISBN	1 84362 818 X
Melodie the Music Fairy	ISBN	1 84362 819 8
Grace the Glitter Fairy	ISBN	1 84362 820 1
Honey the Sweet Fairy	ISBN	1 84362 821 X
Polly the Party Fun Fairy	ISBN	1 84362 822 8
Phoebe the Fashion Fairy	ISBN	1 84362 823 6
Jasmine the Present Fairy	ISBN	1 84362 824 4

The Jewel Fairies

India the Moonstone Fairy	ISBN	1 84362 958 5
Scarlett the Garnet Fairy	ISBN	1 84362 954 2
Emily the Emerald Fairy	ISBN	1 84362 955 0
Chloe the Topaz Fairy	ISBN	1 84362 956 9
Amy the Amethyst Fairy	ISBN	1 84362 957 7
Sophie the Sapphire Fairy	ISBN	1 84362 953 4
Lucy the Diamond Fairy	ISBN	1 84362 959 3

The Pet Keeper Fairies

Katie the Kitten Fairy	ISBN	1 84616 166 5
Bella the Bunny Fairy	ISBN	1 84616 170 3
Georgia the Guinea Pig Fairy	ISBN	1 84616 168 1
Lauren the Puppy Fairy	ISBN	1 84616 169 X
Harriet the Hamster Fairy	ISBN	1 84616 167 3
Molly the Goldfish Fairy	ISBN	1 84616 172 X
Penny the Pony Fairy	ISBN	1 84616 171 1

The Fun Day Fairies

Megan the Monday Fairy	ISBN	1 84616 188 6
Tallulah the Tuesday Fairy	ISBN	1 84616 189 4
Willow the Wednesday Fairy	ISBN	1 84616 190 8
Thea the Thursday Fairy	ISBN	1 84616 191 6
Freya the Friday Fairy	ISBN	1 84616 192 4
Sienna the Saturday Fairy	ISBN	1 84616 193 2
Sarah the Sunday Fairy	ISBN	1 84616 194 0

Holly the Christmas Fairy	ISBN	1 84362 661 6
Summer the Holiday Fairy	ISBN	1 84362 960 7
Stella the Star Fairy	ISBN	1 84362 869 4
Kylie the Carnival Fairy	ISBN	1 84616 175 4
The Rainbow Magic Treasury	ISBN	1 84616 047 2

Coming soon:

Paige the Pantomime Fairy	ISBN	1 84616 209 2

All priced at £3.99. *Holly the Christmas Fairy, Summer the Holiday Fairy, Stella the Star Fairy* and *Kylie the Carnival Fairy* are priced at £5.99. *The Rainbow Magic Treasury* is priced at £12.99.
Rainbow Magic books are available from all good bookshops, or can be ordered direct from the publisher: Orchard Books, PO BOX 29, Douglas IM99 1BQ
Credit card orders please telephone 01624 836000
or fax 01624 837033 or visit our Internet site: www.wattspub.co.uk
or e-mail: bookshop@enterprise.net for details.

To order please quote title, author and ISBN and your full name and address.
Cheques and postal orders should be made payable to 'Bookpost plc.'
Postage and packing is FREE within the UK
(overseas customers should add £2.00 per book).
Prices and availability are subject to change.

Look out for the Petal Fairies!

Tia
the Tulip
Fairy

TIA THE TULIP FAIRY
1-84616-457-5

Pippa
the Poppy
Fairy

PIPPA THE POPPY FAIRY
1-84616-458-3

Louise
the Lily
Fairy

LOUISE THE LILY FAIRY
1-84616-459-1

Charlotte
the sunflower
fairy

CHARLOTTE THE
SUNFLOWER FAIRY
1-84616-460-5

Olivia
the Orchid
Fairy

OLIVIA THE ORCHID FAIRY
1-84616-461-3

Danielle
the Daisy
Fairy

DANIELLE THE DAISY FAIRY
1-84616-462-1

Ella
the Rose
Fairy

ELLA THE ROSE FAIRY
1-84616-464-8

Available from
Thursday 5th April 2007